LOVE you ALWAYS

For Annie and Harriet. Always. F.S.
For Joanne. M.B.

First published 2019 by Nosy Crow Ltd
The Crow's Nest, 14 Baden Place
Crosby Row, London SE1 1YW
www.nosycrow.com

ISBN 978 1 78800 522 7 (HB)
ISBN 978 1 78800 523 4 (PB)

Nosy Crow and associated logos are trademarks
and/or registered trademarks of Nosy Crow Ltd

Text © Frances Stickley 2019
Illustrations © Migy Blanco 2019

The right of Frances Stickley to be identified as the author
and Migy Blanco to be identified as the illustrator of this work has been asserted.

A CIP catalogue record for this book is available from the British Library.

Printed in China

Papers used by Nosy Crow are made from wood
grown in sustainable forests.

1 3 5 7 9 8 6 4 2 (HB)
1 3 5 7 9 8 6 4 2 (PB)

LOVE YOU ALWAYS

Frances Stickley & Migy Blanco

nosy crow

Hoglet and his mummy snuffled home beneath the trees.
The leaves were rustling softly in the gentle autumn breeze.

Little Hoglet shivered as the leaves came drifting down.

"Everything feels **different** now,"
said Hoglet with a frown.

"Everything is changing," Mummy said. "It's nature's way.
But change makes nature lovelier with every passing day."

Hoglet looked around him and he suddenly felt strange.
"Mummy . . .

would you love me **more**," he wondered, "if I changed?"

"Would you love me **more**
if I could dart across the leaves?
What if I was like a squirrel
dashing through the trees?"

"Imagine that," said Mummy.
"How exciting it would seem,
but I couldn't love you more
if you could race the rushing stream."

"Would you love me **more** if I could fly up in the sky?
What if I could flutter like a dainty dragonfly?"

"Imagine that," said Mummy.
"How you'd sparkle, little one,
but I couldn't love you more
if you could soar up to the sun."

"Would you love me **more** if I could leap along a log?
What if I could bounce across the lilies like a frog?"

"Imagine that," said Mummy. "What a joy to jump so high,
but I couldn't love you more if you could spring into the sky."

"Would you love me **more** if I had smooth and silky hair?
What if I was fluffy like the rabbits over there?"

"Imagine that," said Mummy.
"Fur or prickles, I'd be proud,
but I couldn't love you more
if you were softer than a cloud."

"But Mummy," Hoglet wondered, "will love always last forever, even if I change just like the seasons or the weather?"

"Always," Mummy said.
"As long as skies are high above,

there's one thing that will never change,"
she promised . . .

. . . "and that's love."

"I'll love you **always,** little one. I've loved you from the start.
I'll tell you every day, until you know the words by heart."

"Always," whispered Hoglet
as he curled up in his bed.
"Imagine that," he murmured . . .

. . . "Just imagine," Mummy said.